WEEKS
GREENLAND, N. H

W9-CMS-793

# JENNIFER ARMSTRONG
# CHIN YU MIN AND THE GINGER CAT

*illustrated by* MARY GRANDPRÉ

CROWN PUBLISHERS, INC. • *New York*

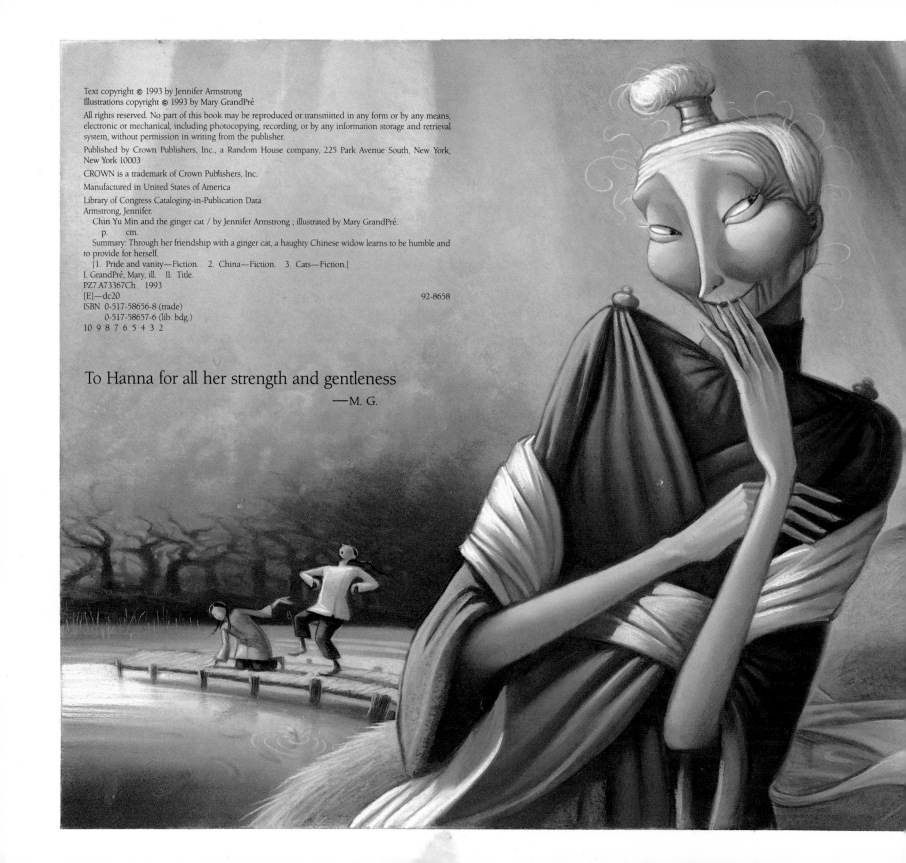

Text copyright © 1993 by Jennifer Armstrong
Illustrations copyright © 1993 by Mary GrandPré

All rights reserved. No part of this book may be reproduced or transmitted in any form or by any means, electronic or mechanical, including photocopying, recording, or by any information storage and retrieval system, without permission in writing from the publisher.

Published by Crown Publishers, Inc., a Random House company, 225 Park Avenue South, New York, New York 10003

CROWN is a trademark of Crown Publishers, Inc.

Manufactured in United States of America

Library of Congress Cataloging-in-Publication Data
Armstrong, Jennifer.
   Chin Yu Min and the ginger cat / by Jennifer Armstrong ; illustrated by Mary GrandPré.
      p.    cm.
   Summary: Through her friendship with a ginger cat, a haughty Chinese widow learns to be humble and to provide for herself.
   [1. Pride and vanity—Fiction.   2. China—Fiction.   3. Cats—Fiction.]
I. GrandPré, Mary, ill.   II. Title.
PZ7.A73367Ch   1993
[E]—dc20                                                          92-8658
ISBN  0-517-58656-8 (trade)
        0-517-58657-6 (lib. bdg.)
10 9 8 7 6 5 4 3 2

To Hanna for all her strength and gentleness

—M. G.

**M**any years ago, in a village near Kunming, there lived an official of the government named Secretary Chin. In his house by the lake were the finest lacquer bowls, lettered scrolls of the sheerest paper, and many, many strings of cash. Secretary Chin was very prosperous.

The wife of this man, Chin Yu Min, felt that this prosperity was only what she deserved. She was proud and haughty, and she made her servants perform impossible and meaningless tasks—such as collecting incense smoke in a bamboo cage or teaching carp to strut like roosters— just for the fun of displaying her power. She laughed at beggars and turned them away from her door.

One day Secretary Chin fell out of his small yellow pleasure boat and sank like a piece of carved jade to the bottom of the lake. That was the end of Secretary Chin, and it was also the end of his wife's idleness and luxury.

"Good Chin Yu Min," said her neighbors. "Please allow us to help you in this time of loss."

"Aiyi!" Chin Yu Min scoffed. "I don't need help from such as you. Be off!"

She slammed the door in their faces and stomped away. For many months Chin Yu Min scolded her servants and haggled suspiciously with the merchants. She was sure that everyone was out to cheat her, and she answered their pleasant words with bitter ones.

Coin by square-holed coin, her strings of cash flowed away like streams from a fishpond. Chin Yu Min knew she would soon be poor, but she would rather have eaten ashes than let anyone know of this fact.

"Aiyi!" Chin Yu Min screamed at her servants. "You are all less than useless! Leave my house!" When they had gone, she lived alone and tended house with her own hands to save money.

"Esteemed Chin Yu Min," said her neighbors. "Allow us to help you."

"Who asked for your help?" Chin Yu Min retorted.

She slammed the door in their faces and stomped away.

Chin Yu Min lived alone for several more months, becoming poorer and poorer. At last she was as poor as a mouse in a monastery.

Not one chicken scratched in her yard. Her rice jar stood cracked and empty. The fine lacquer bowls were dulled by hard use, and the lettered scrolls of sheerest paper flapped like ragged ghosts from the walls.

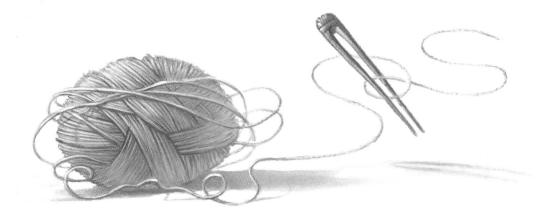

One morning when Chin Yu Min awoke, she knew there was not a thing in the house to eat. She knew there was no cash with which to buy rice.

"I will fish," Chin Yu Min announced to her empty house and the tattered scrolls.

With this decision firmly made, Chin Yu Min took a string and a hairpin for a hook and went to the lake. She stood straight and aloof, arms out, eyes forward, line dangling, and waited—oh, for only a little while—before scowling with impatience.

"There are no fish in this lake!" she complained.

But below the surface of the water many fish indeed shuttled back and forth like monkeys at play in the treetops. Chin Yu Min shook her fist at the fish and called them uncivil names.

Then a melodious splash caught her ear.

"Aiyi!" Chin Yu Min whispered.

On the next dock sat a fine ginger cat. He draped his long elegant tail into the water, and

*flick!*

Out it came with a fish biting the end. The cat regarded the fish with a solemn look, blinked, and then quickly ate every bit, scales, fins, and all.

"Oh, Peerless Ginger Cat!" said Chin Yu Min. "Catch a fish for me!"

The ginger cat blinked his eyes. "Certainly, Auntie."

He draped his long elegant tail into the water, and

*flick!*

Out it came with a fish on the end.

Chin Yu Min picked it up and sniffed deeply. "Steamed with ginger and soy sauce, this will be delicious."

Chin Yu Min hurried back to her house with the fish and put it on to cook. But as the aromatic steam curled up around her gray-haired head, Chin Yu Min began to worry.

"I have a fish today, but what will I have tomorrow?" she asked herself.

She peeked out the window. The ginger cat was still sitting on the dock, meditating on a pair of mandarin ducks who swam in graceful harmony through the reeds.

Chin Yu Min had an idea.

"Oh, Gracious Ginger Cat!" the greedy woman said, joining him on the dock. "My house is large, my bed is soft. Why not come and live with me? There you will be safe from dogs, cool in the summer, and warm in the winter. All I ask is that you continue to catch fish."

"I thank you, Venerable Auntie," said the cat. "I accept your offer. You are truly generous."

Chin Yu Min smiled a thin smile and hurried back to her house.

From that day Chin Yu Min's prosperity returned. Surely, her neighbors agreed, she had found a charm to make fish jump from the lake into her basket, for every day she arrived at the market with a load of glittering, glistening fish. Her neighbors looked on as Chin Yu Min hung new scrolls with the characters of "Wise Decision" and "Good Management" on her door, and admired the new lacquer bowls that she bought from the merchants. Chin Yu Min was prosperous indeed.

Every day in the afternoon the ginger cat sat on the dock and draped his long elegant tail into the water, and

*flick!*

He pulled out fish after fish until they were piled up like the mountains of Guilin. Chin Yu Min rubbed her hands together and counted her strings of cash.

"Auntie," said the ginger cat one day. "What would you do if I went away?"

"Aiyi!" gasped Chin Yu Min. "Don't leave me! How would I eat?"

Chin Yu Min wrung her hands. She could not bear another plunge into poverty.

"I will stay, Auntie," replied the ginger cat.

In the evenings of the warm months Chin Yu Min sat in front of her door watching the lake with the ginger cat at her side. From time to time the sound of his purring broke the stillness, and Chin Yu Min was content as she watched the cranes fly overhead.

In the evenings of the cool months Chin Yu Min sat in front of a fire in the house watching the coals with the ginger cat at her side. From time to time the sound of his purring broke the stillness, and Chin Yu Min was content as she watched the embers glow at her feet.

"Auntie," said the ginger cat one day. "What would you do if I went away?"

"Aiyi!" gasped Chin Yu Min. She hastily stroked his back. "Don't do that to an old woman!"

Chin Yu Min wrung her hands. She could not bear another plunge into solitude.

"I will stay, Auntie," replied the ginger cat.

One day a beggar came to the door.

"Please, Virtuous Lady," he said. "Have you an old basket in which I may carry my meager belongings?"

"Pah!" said Chin Yu Min. "Filthy beggar! There, take that ragged thing. It's of no use to me."

So saying, she pointed at a torn and tattered basket that lay discarded in the sun.

"Blessings upon you," the beggar said. He hoisted the basket above his head and limped off to town.

Chin Yu Min cast a thoughtful glance out at the lake. It was time for the ginger cat to start fishing for the day.

"Honorable Ginger Cat!" she called out. "Where are you?"

The answer was wind soughing through the trees.

"Delightful Ginger Cat!" she called again. "Where are you?"

The answer was wavelets lapping the pebbled shore. The ginger cat was nowhere.

"He has left me!" Chin Yu Min cried out.

She stood stricken in the doorway, staring at her fine scrolls. "Wise Decision" and "Good Management" mocked her as they rustled in the breeze.

"No more fish!" Chin Yu Min despaired.

The scrolls rustled again.

"No more prosperity!"

The scrolls shivered.

"No more sitting by the fire!"

The scrolls flapped forlornly.

"No more purring!"

The scrolls fell from their hooks.

"No more fine ginger cat to sit beside me!"

Chin Yu Min tore at her hair. "Wise Decision" and "Good Management" lay in shreds at her feet. In despair Chin Yu Min took up a brush and wrote the characters for "Bottomless Sorrow" on her door.

"Have you seen my ginger cat?" Chin Yu Min asked the neighbors. "Help me find my ginger cat!"

Her neighbors frowned. "When we offered you our help, Chin Yu Min, you scorned us."

"I beseech you," Chin Yu Min said. "Most humbly I ask, have you seen my ginger cat?"

"We have not," her neighbors said, taking pity on her bottomless sorrow. "But we have seen a beggar with an old basket pass this way. Perhaps he knows something."

Chin Yu Min stood as still as a plum tree, rooted to the ground. As sure as the sun rose and set, she knew that the ginger cat had been sleeping in the basket. She had given him away.

"Where, oh, where has the beggar gone?" Chin Yu Min asked her neighbors.

"To the market," they replied.

Chin Yu Min ran as fast as her skinny old legs would carry her to the market. There, to her amazement, she found many, many beggars, each with a tattered basket. To her, all beggars looked alike, because she had always been too proud to see their faces.

Now she did not know which one had her basket.

"I beg you," she said to the first. "Venerable Old Monk. Allow me to buy your basket."

The beggar bowed once and pulled on his thin gray beard. "For ten cash, madam."

Chin Yu Min gritted her teeth. But her ginger cat was worth more than that in fish. She paid the beggar and snatched the basket: empty.

"I beg you," she said to the next. "Spiritual Old Monk. Allow me to buy your basket."

The beggar bowed once and tugged his short stubby beard. "For ten cash, madam."

Chin Yu Min gritted her teeth. But her ginger cat was worth more than that in fish. She paid the beggar and snatched the basket: empty.

"I beg you," she said to the third. "Self-Denying Old Monk. Allow me to buy your basket."

Before each beggar she humbled herself and paid for the baskets. Her strings of cash were vanishing like water into sand. The longer she searched for her cat, the more desolate she became.

"For ten cash," said another beggar.

Chin Yu Min pulled at her hair. But all the fish in the Middle Kingdom were not equal to her ginger cat. He was worth far, far more in companionship and warmth.

"Ten cash," said the next.

"Ten cash," said another.

At last she had not one single coin left, and Chin Yu Min was as poor as the beggars—even poorer, for each of them had ten cash, and she had none. But more bitter than the loss of her cash was the loss of her cat.

"Let him not catch another fish!" she cried to heaven. "But still let my friend come back to live with me!"

In tears, Chin Yu Min turned away from the market and trod wearily back to the lake. But before she reached her home, she saw another beggar ahead on the road. This beggar, too, had an old basket.

"Most Scholarly Old Monk," cried the proud Chin Yu Min. "Pity an old woman as poor as you! I beg you to give me your basket."

Chin Yu Min knelt in the road and kowtowed with her forehead to the dust. Her heart cried out for the ginger cat.

"Certainly, madam," the beggar said. "If I can take away your bottomless sorrow in this way, I will give you my basket."

So saying, he placed the basket on the ground beside her and hobbled away.

Fear shook Chin Yu Min's hands as she opened the basket. Her breath quaked in her throat.

Inside, curled in sleep, was the ginger cat.

"Oh, Generous Friend!" Chin Yu Min cried. "I have found you again!"

"Good afternoon, Auntie," said the ginger cat, stretching his legs. "Isn't it time to fish?"

For her answer Chin Yu Min hugged the cat to her heart.

"Today I fish for you," she said.

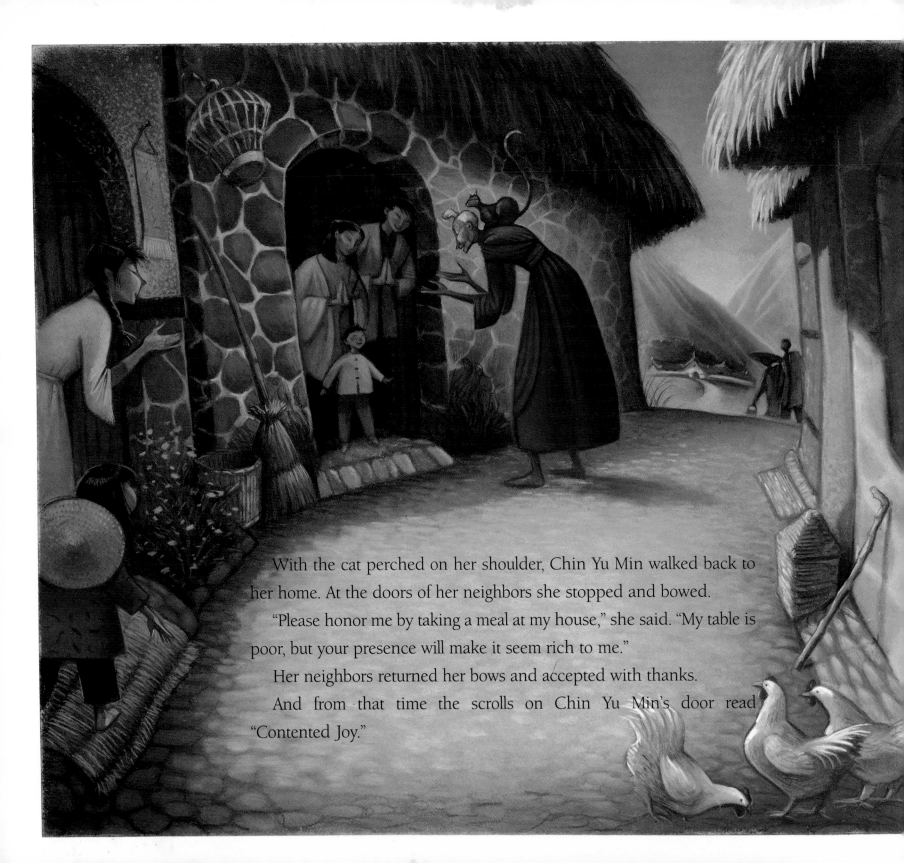

With the cat perched on her shoulder, Chin Yu Min walked back to her home. At the doors of her neighbors she stopped and bowed.

"Please honor me by taking a meal at my house," she said. "My table is poor, but your presence will make it seem rich to me."

Her neighbors returned her bows and accepted with thanks.

And from that time the scrolls on Chin Yu Min's door read "Contented Joy."